MINNESOTA
TWINS

by Joe Bissen

Published by ABDO Publishing Company, 8000 West 78th Street, Edina, Minnesota 55439. Copyright © 2011 by Abdo Consulting Group, Inc. International copyrights reserved in all countries. No part of this book may be reproduced in any form without written permission from the publisher. SportsZone™ is a trademark and logo of ABDO Publishing Company.

Printed in the United States of America,
North Mankato, Minnesota
112010
012011

Editor: Matt Tustison
Copy Editor: Nicholas Cafarelli
Interior Design and Production: Craig Hinton
Cover Design: Craig Hinton

Photo Credits: Paul Sancya/AP Images, cover; Otto Greule/Allsport/Getty Images, title; John Swart/AP Images, 4; Jim Mone/AP Images, 7, 26, 28, 31; Rusty Kennedy/AP Images, 8, 44; Peter Southwick/AP Images, 11, 43 (top); AP Images, 12, 15, 20, 25, 42 (top and bottom); Gene Herrick/AP Images, 16, 42 (middle); Photo by Herb Scharfman/Sports Imagery/Getty Images, 19; Photo by Focus on Sport/Getty Images, 22; Mark Duncan, File/AP Images, 32, 43 (middle); Tom Olmscheid/AP Images, 34; Kathy Willens/AP Images, 37; Photo by Genevieve Ross/Getty Images, 38; Ann Heisenfelt/AP Images, 41, 43 (bottom); Paul Battaglia/AP Images, 47

Library of Congress Cataloging-in-Publication Data
Bissen, Joe, 1957-
 Minnesota Twins / Joe Bissen.
   p. cm. — (Inside MLB)
 Includes index.
 ISBN 978-1-61714-050-1
 1. Minnesota Twins (Baseball team)—History—Juvenile literature. I. Title.
 GV875.M55B57 2011
 796.357'6409776578—dc22
                        2010036569

TABLE OF CONTENTS

CHAPTER 1

MAKING SOME NOISE

What is the loudest noise you have ever heard? A train barreling down the tracks? A jackhammer tearing up a city street? A jet airplane roaring as it takes off?

Those are all extremely loud noises. But to many of the 55,293 sports fans who were in the Hubert H. Humphrey Metrodome in Minneapolis on the afternoon of October 24, 1987, the sound of a baseball game is probably the loudest noise they have ever heard.

The home team, the Minnesota Twins, was facing the St. Louis Cardinals that day in

Home Cooking

The Twins had a remarkable record in home games in 1987. They won 56 games and lost only 25 in the Metrodome during the regular season. The Twins won both of their home games on the way to beating the Detroit Tigers in five games in the American League Championship Series (ALCS). Minnesota then won all four games that were held in the Metrodome in the World Series, helping the Twins outlast the St. Louis Cardinals in seven games.

Kent Hrbek celebrates after hitting a grand slam during the Twins' 11–5 victory over the Cardinals in Game 6 of the 1987 World Series.

Game 6 of the World Series. The first team to win four games in the Series would win baseball's world championship. The Cardinals were on the verge of capturing the title. They led the Series three games to two and needed to win only one of the last two games.

But the Twins were leading this sixth game, by a narrow 6–5

Bert Blyleven

Bert Blyleven had one of the best curveballs in major league history. Blyleven spun his "hook," as a curveball is sometimes called, for 22 seasons in the major leagues. He was only 19 years old as a rookie with the Twins in 1970. He won 15 games or more seven times with Minnesota. He went 3–1 in the postseason as the Twins won the 1987 world championship. Blyleven won 287 career games pitching mostly for mediocre teams. Through 2010, he ranked fifth all time in strikeouts with 3,701. As of 2010, he was not in the Baseball Hall of Fame, though he came very close to receiving enough votes that year.

margin, as they came to bat in the bottom of the sixth inning. Greg Gagne singled, and then Kirby Puckett walked. With one out, Don Baylor was walked intentionally. Tom Brunansky then popped out.

The bases were loaded. There were two outs. Up to the plate strode Kent Hrbek. The burly Twins slugger grew up about 10 miles (16 km) from the Metrodome. He had a chance to be a World Series hero for his hometown team. Minnesota fans roared, furiously waving their "Homer Hankies." The little white-and-red handkerchiefs symbolized their fanatic support for the Twins.

The first pitch from Cardinals reliever Ken Dayley was right where Hrbek wanted it—a fastball over the outside half of the plate. Hrbek took a mighty swing. And he connected. The ball soared toward the stands

Frank Viola delivers a pitch during Game 7 of the 1987 World Series. Minnesota turned to its ace in the crucial game against St. Louis.

in center field and landed 439 feet from home plate. It was a mammoth blast—a grand slam home run. It gave the Twins a 10–5 lead, and it gave them breathing room.

At the time, it was the most important home run in Twins history. "The run around the bases didn't last long enough," Hrbek said. "I wanted to do it a couple more times. The noise was incredible."

What a noise it was. The Metrodome crowd noise during the 1987 World Series was estimated to be as loud as the sound a jet makes when taking off. It was so loud that one of the devices used to measure

the noise broke. It was so loud that coaches sitting next to the bullpen telephones, waiting for managers' orders to warm up relief pitchers, could not even hear the phones ring.

The Twins went on to an 11–5 victory, setting up the most dramatic event possible in baseball: Game 7 of the World Series.

Frank Viola was the man on the mound for the Twins in Game 7. The left-hander known as "Sweet Music" was the Twins' best pitcher that year. He won 17 games in the regular season. He also won Game 4 of the ALCS over the Detroit Tigers and Game 1 of the World Series.

Game 7 did not start well for Viola, however. The Twins fell behind 2–0 in the second

A Long Wait

The 1987 World Series championship meant a lot to Minnesota sports fans. They had waited a long time for something like it. The Twins had not been in a World Series since 1965, when they lost to the Los Angeles Dodgers. The football Vikings had been to four Super Bowls, and lost them all. The hockey North Stars had lost in their only two appearances in the Stanley Cup Finals, in 1981 and 1991. You had to go all the way back to 1954, when the Minneapolis Lakers won the NBA championship, to find a Minnesota team that had won a championship in a major professional sport.

inning. But they were resilient. They were battlers the whole season, making it to the World Series despite going only 85–77 in the regular season—a record not usually good enough to make the postseason.

Puckett tied the score at 2–2 with a run-scoring double in the fifth inning. Gagne put

Players, including Roy Smalley, *wearing cap*, celebrate the Twins' Game 7 win in the 1987 World Series. The title was the franchise's first in Minnesota.

KIRBY PUCKETT

Kirby Puckett was a great ballplayer. The statistics say so. Puckett had four hits in his first major league game in 1984. He had 10 hits in 11 at-bats in a three-game series at Milwaukee in 1987. He finished his career with a .318 batting average. Puckett was a skilled bunter who could hit for power, too. He hit 207 home runs. He could hit a ball pitched anywhere. When he manned center field, he leaped above fences to rob opponents of home runs.

But more than that, Puckett was a great teammate. "He was the best teammate I've ever been around," said Andy MacPhail, the Twins' general manager during Puckett's playing days.

But tragedy followed Puckett, too. He had to retire from baseball in 1996 after losing the sight in his right eye because of a condition called glaucoma. He died of a massive stroke on March 6, 2006, at age 45.

Minnesota ahead 3–2 with a single in the sixth. Dan Gladden drove in another run for the Twins with a double in the eighth. Meanwhile, Viola was mowing the Cardinals down. He held them scoreless from the third through eighth innings.

With the Twins leading 4–2, relief pitcher Jeff Reardon took over in the ninth. Reardon was known as "The Terminator" for the way he shut down opponents and finished games. Reardon retired the side 1–2–3 to give the Twins their first world championship. The Twins swarmed Reardon on the pitching mound.

Minnesotans celebrated for days, wrapping up with a parade through the streets of downtown Minneapolis and St. Paul. Puckett, a superstar center fielder who always

Twins center fielder Kirby Puckett, *left*, and closer Jeff Reardon acknowledge the home crowd after the Twins won the 1987 World Series.

made people laugh, wore a mile-wide grin and an old aviator's cap in the parade, making him look like a 1920s airplane pilot.

Twins third baseman Gary Gaetti knew the 1987 season provided moments that would last a lifetime. "When I'm 65 years old," he said, "I'm going to take my grandchild to his first baseball game. We'll take our seats, and I'll say to him, 'Baseball is the national pastime, the greatest game in the world. And the greatest thing you can do in baseball is win a World Series.' Then I'll pause and say, 'I once played for a World Series winner.'"

CHAPTER 2

WHERE IT ALL STARTED

Before the team became the Minnesota Twins, it was the Washington Senators. The Senators joined the American League (AL) in 1901 and played in Washington DC through 1960.

The Senators franchise was founded in 1894 as the Kansas City Blues in Missouri. The Blues played in the Western League, which was a minor league. In 1900, the Western League changed its name to the AL. The next year, the AL gained major league status, joining the National League (NL) in that regard. Also in 1901, the Blues moved to Washington DC, the nation's capital, and became the Senators. There were eight teams, including the Senators, in the AL's first year as a major league.

The Senators were not very good. In 60 years of existence, they won only three AL pennants. Yet as bad as the Senators were, they did have two consecutive outstanding seasons.

Walter Johnson, shown in 1924, was a legendary pitcher for the Washington Senators. The Senators played in the AL from 1901 to 1960 before moving to Minnesota and becoming the Twins.

"BIG TRAIN"

Walter Johnson, a dominant pitcher for the Washington Senators from 1907 to 1927, was one of the five original members of the Baseball Hall of Fame. He was elected in 1936, along with Ty Cobb, Christy Mathewson, Babe Ruth, and Honus Wagner.

Johnson's nickname was "Big Train." He had a great fastball that looked like it was thrown out of a slingshot. Johnson put together a remarkable 36–7 record in 1913. Through 2010, his 417 victories ranked second to Cy Young's 511 on baseball's all-time list. He also was ninth in strikeouts (3,509) and 10th in earned-run average (2.17). He was the major league record-holder with 110 shutouts and fifth in complete games with 531. Johnson led the AL in strikeouts a record 12 times.

After his playing days, Johnson managed the Senators from 1929 to 1932 and the Cleveland Indians from 1933 to 1935.

In 1924, they finished 92–62 and won the World Series over the New York Giants. Earl McNeely hit a run-scoring double in the bottom of the 12th inning of Game 7 to give Washington its only world championship. Star pitcher Walter Johnson worked the last four innings in relief. The next year, the Senators won 96 games and the AL pennant. But they fell in the World Series in seven games to the Pittsburgh Pirates.

The Senators also had a strong season in 1933. They finished a team-best 99–53 and made it to the World Series. However, they lost in five games to the Giants.

Despite its overall struggles, Washington did have some talent. Several players who would be enshrined in the Baseball Hall of Fame spent at least a portion of their careers

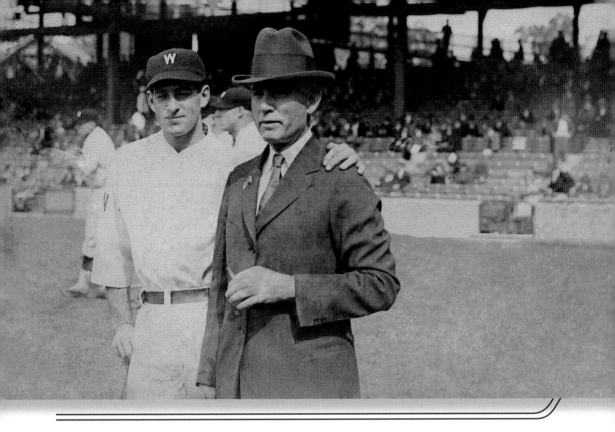

Senators manager Bucky Harris, *left*, poses with owner Clark Griffith at the 1924 World Series. The Senators beat the New York Giants in seven games.

with the Senators. Some—such as Johnson (1907–27) and outfielders Sam Rice (1915–33) and Goose Goslin (1921–29, 1938)—played for Washington for many years. The team also had a Hall of Fame manager in Bucky Harris (1924–28, 1935–42, 1950–54).

However, in general, the Senators had bad teams. From 1954 through 1960, they never had a winning season. The team was struggling on the field and off of it. It lost money because it could not draw enough fans. Soon enough, the Senators would pack up and move halfway across the country.

CHAPTER 3

A MOVE UP

By the 1950s, fans stopped coming to Washington Senators games. The team lost money consistently. Owner Calvin Griffith finally decided it was time to leave the nation's capital.

The Senators and Minnesota became a match. Minnesota had a stadium, Metropolitan Stadium in the Minneapolis suburb of Bloomington, that was ready to be a home for a major league team. Baseball fans in Minnesota were ready to pay to watch big-league baseball.

On October 26, 1960, AL team owners voted to allow Griffith to move his Senators to Minnesota. They were renamed "the Twins" in honor of Minnesota's Twin Cities of Minneapolis and St. Paul. They played their first game on April 11, 1961. Pedro Ramos pitched a three-hitter as Minnesota shut out the mighty New York Yankees 6–0 at Yankee Stadium.

The Twins won a very respectable 91 games in both

Washington Senators owner Calvin Griffith, *raising his cap*, is welcomed to Minnesota in November 1960. Griffith's relocated team became the Minnesota Twins.

Tony Oliva

For all the power Harmon Killebrew generated, his teammate Tony Oliva might have been a better "pure" hitter. In other words, Oliva made contact more often, hit more line drives, and still had power. In 1964, Oliva batted .323 and became the first rookie to win the AL batting championship. He won two more batting titles and hit .300 or better five more times. Sadly, late in his career he wound up with bad knees. They limited his effectiveness and shortened his career. If he could have stayed healthy, he almost certainly would have made the Baseball Hall of Fame.

1962 and 1963. More importantly, they had developed outstanding players. Infielder Harmon Killebrew muscled 46 home runs in 1961. He added 48, 45, and 49 homers the next three seasons. Outfielder Bob Allison added more power. Jim Kaat, Camilo Pascual, and Jim "Mudcat" Grant were reliable pitchers. Tony Oliva, a native of Cuba, came on board in 1964.

He immediately became one of baseball's best outfielders.

By 1965, the pieces were in place for a run at the AL pennant. But first, the Twins needed to develop just a bit more of a winning character. An incident in spring training made a big difference.

Zoilo Versalles, a shortstop with talent but not always the best attitude, failed to hustle on a ground ball hit to him. Manager Sam Mele pulled him out of the game and ordered him to run sprints. Versalles was upset and said he would play hard for the team's new third-base coach, Billy Martin. Mele insisted that Versalles also play hard for him and fined him $300. Versalles got the message and changed his attitude. He became the key player as the Twins went an astounding 102–60 and won the AL pennant by seven games.

Tony Oliva swings during Game 1 of the 1965 World Series at Metropolitan Stadium. The Twins lost the Series in seven games to the Dodgers.

Versalles hit 45 doubles, scored 126 runs, and was named AL Most Valuable Player (MVP). Oliva hit .321. Grant won 21 games and Kaat 18. Despite injuries to Killebrew, Allison, and Pascual and an illness to pitcher Dave Boswell, the Twins would face the Los Angeles Dodgers in the World Series.

The Dodgers, though, had too much pitching power for the Twins in the World Series. Even though Grant and Kaat

Man of Gold

Besides being one of the Twins' best pitchers ever, Jim Kaat was one of the best fielders ever for any team. "Kitty," as he was nicknamed, won a Gold Glove Award as his league's best-fielding pitcher for 16 consecutive seasons.

Harmon Killebrew connects for one of his major league-best 49 homers in 1969. The slugger also led the big leagues with 140 RBIs that season.

outpitched Dodgers superstars Don Drysdale and Sandy Koufax to help the Twins win the first two games at home, Los Angeles came back. Koufax, pitching on just two days of rest in Game 7, outdueled Kaat 2–0 at Metropolitan Stadium to give the Dodgers the world championship.

The Twins finished second in the AL in 1966 and 1967. They dropped to seventh in 1968. Cal Ermer was fired as manager, and Minnesota named Martin as its new manager. Martin had a terrible temper. But he usually got a lot out of his players.

Martin's 1969 Twins team won 97 games. His 1970 team won 98. Each won the new AL West Division. Beginning in 1969, the AL and the NL reorganized into leagues with two divisions each. They began playing an extra round of the playoffs before the World Series known as the championship series.

The Twins' style of play under Martin, hustling and aggressive, became known as "Billy Ball." Their young second baseman, Rod Carew, hit .332 in 1969 to lead the AL. He also stole home seven times, matching a major league record.

Minnesota had power, as well. Oliva hit better than .300 in 1969 and 1970. Killebrew smashed a combined 90 home runs in those two seasons. In 1969, he hit 49 homers, drove in 140 runs, and won the AL MVP Award. But the Twins' postseason efforts were not so great. In both 1969 and 1970, they were swept by the Baltimore Orioles in three games in the ALCS.

HARMON KILLEBREW

Harmon Killebrew did not hit plain old home runs. He hit mile-high blasts that seemed to rise majestically into the stratosphere before settling into the bleachers. "The homers he hit against us," said former Baltimore Orioles manager Paul Richards, "would be homers in any park—including Yellowstone."

Killebrew hit 573 homers in 22 major league seasons. When he retired in 1975, he ranked fifth on baseball's all-time home-run list. He led the AL in homers six times.

One of his hitting coaches, Ralph Rowe, explained where Killebrew's power came from. "Look at those wrists," Rowe said. "Look how thick they are, how powerful."

Killebrew was nicknamed "The Killer," even though that did not fit his personality. He was humble and did not brag.

CHAPTER 4

THE DOWN YEARS

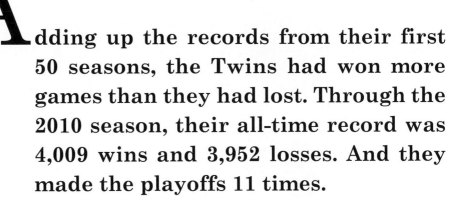

A dding up the records from their first 50 seasons, the Twins had won more games than they had lost. Through the 2010 season, their all-time record was 4,009 wins and 3,952 losses. And they made the playoffs 11 times.

But things went wrong in those 50 seasons, too. After winning the AL West in 1970, the rest of the 1970s turned into the Dark Ages for the Twins. They finished fifth in the West the next season. They then never finished better than third for the rest of the decade.

What went wrong? Plenty. The decline started with Billy Martin's firing as manager after the 1970 season. Martin was outstanding as an on-the-field manager. But he had a prickly personality. He often went against the orders of team owner Calvin Griffith, who got tired of it all and fired Martin.

Minnesota fans were upset with the decision. Many stopped going to games. Griffith began

Billy Martin, shown in 1969, led the Twins to division titles in both of his years as manager. But he and owner Calvin Griffith did not get along, and Martin was fired after the 1970 season. Minnesota then began to struggle.

saying he could not afford to pay the high salaries that star players were earning.

Then came a watershed moment in sports history. Curt Flood, a big-league outfielder, sued baseball in 1970. Flood opposed the "reserve clause," which bound a player to one team for his entire career, unless he was traded. Flood believed that a player should be allowed to sign with any team he wanted to once his contract ended. It took until 1975 for players to win "free agency" rights. But Flood's lawsuit had changed the game forever.

Griffith could not have liked free agency. He was not as rich as many other team owners. Griffith knew the game. But that was not enough. His coaches and scouts helped develop talented young players such as Lyman Bostock, Dave Goltz, and Bill Campbell. But that also was not enough.

Griffith complained constantly that players' salaries were too high. It was like a row of dominoes for the Twins in the 1970s. Once the collapse started, there was no stopping it. Tony Oliva suffered severe knee injuries and could barely run by the mid-1970s. Griffith even battled Harmon Killebrew

Rod Carew, shown in 1978, starred for Minnesota from 1967 to 1978. He was an All-Star all 12 of those seasons and won seven batting titles.

over salaries. Killebrew signed with the Kansas City Royals in 1975.

Griffith traded star pitcher Bert Blyleven and promising shortstop Danny Thompson to the Texas Rangers in 1976. The Twins' decline continued.

In September 1978, Griffith went too far. He gave a speech to a group in Waseca, Minnesota. He made nasty comments about catcher Butch Wynegar and, speaking to an all-white audience, racist comments about African Americans.

Griffith apologized. But his star player, Rod Carew, a black man, was furious. Carew said he would never play another

Calvin Griffith, *left*, and Carl Pohlad are shown in June 1984. Griffith had just turned over ownership of the Twins to Pohlad.

game for Griffith. Carew was dealt to the California Angels on February 3, 1979.

The Twins had their worst season ever in 1982. They won 60 games, lost 102, and finished in last place in the AL West. As Griffith unloaded his veteran players, he saddled his manager, Billy "Slick" Gardner, with 15 rookies. Amid the darkness, there were bright lights. Rookie first baseman Kent Hrbek batted .301 with 23 home runs. Rookie third baseman Gary Gaetti belted 25 homers. Other promising rookies were outfielder Tom Brunansky, outfielder/designated hitter Randy Bush, catcher Tim Laudner, and starting pitcher Frank Viola. All would become key players on the Twins' 1987 World Series championship team.

The end of the Griffith era was near. After threatening to move the team to another state in the early 1980s, he sold the Twins in 1984 to Carl Pohlad, a Minneapolis banker, for $38 million. Two years earlier, the team had moved into a new stadium, the Metrodome. Within 10 years of opening the ballpark, the Twins would have a couple of big celebrations there.

HE HUNG IN THERE

When Jim Eisenreich was a kid, he was teased. Eisenreich's face twitched, and his eyes blinked. Sometimes he made unusual noises. There was nothing he could do about these symptoms, called tics.

Eisenreich was a terrific baseball player. He made it to the big leagues in 1982 with the Twins. Sadly, the teasing did not stop. In a 1982 game at Fenway Park, Boston Red Sox fans jeered him. Eisenreich had to take himself out of the game. He played parts of two more seasons with the Twins, but his tics would not go away.

Finally, in 1986, it was discovered that he had Tourette Syndrome, a condition that causes tics. Eisenreich got medication and a new chance to play with the Kansas City Royals. Eisenreich wound up playing 15 seasons in the big leagues. Today, he speaks to children and their families, helping them understand his disability.

CHAPTER 5

RETURN TO GLORY

After winning the World Series in 1987, the Twins slipped. They won six more games in 1988 than they had in 1987 but finished second in the AL West. They finished fifth in 1989. They ended up in last place, seventh, in 1990.

That set the stage for one of the greatest comebacks in baseball history. The Twins needed leadership and better pitching as they entered the 1991 season. They got both when they signed Jack Morris to a one-year contract. Morris won 162 games for the Detroit Tigers in the 1980s, more than any other big-league pitcher.

Morris, a St. Paul native, could be gruff. But he was determined to win. Starting pitchers Morris, Kevin Tapani, and 23-year-old Scott Erickson combined for 54 wins and only 29 losses. Rick Aguilera was the bullpen star with 42 saves. Kirby Puckett hit .319, and newly signed designated hitter Chili Davis smacked 29 home

Jack Morris pitches during Game 7 of the 1991 World Series. Morris went the distance in leading Minnesota to a 1–0, 10-inning win over Atlanta.

KENT HRBEK

First baseman Kent Hrbek, nicknamed "Herbie," played parts of 14 seasons for the Twins, from 1981 to 1994.

Hrbek grew up in Bloomington, the Minneapolis suburb in which Metropolitan Stadium was located. The Twins selected him in the 17th round of the 1978 amateur draft. The left-handed hitting Hrbek played his first full major league season in 1982 and finished second in the AL Rookie of the Year voting to Baltimore Orioles shortstop Cal Ripken Jr. Hrbek batted .301 with 23 homers and 92 runs batted in (RBIs) and was named an All-Star.

Hrbek, who became huskier as his career went on, hit 20 or more homers in 10 seasons with Minnesota, with a career high of 34 in 1987. He also was an excellent fielding first baseman. Through 2010, Hrbek's 293 career homers and 1,086 RBIs both ranked second in team history to Harmon Killebrew's totals.

runs. On defense, the Twins were the second-best-fielding team in the AL. Manager Tom Kelly was a calm but firm leader.

It was a complete team. The Twins won a team-record 15 consecutive games in June. They finished with 95 wins and won the AL West by eight games.

The Twins dispatched the Toronto Blue Jays in five games in the ALCS. Puckett batted .429. Rookie second baseman Chuck Knoblauch hit .350. That was just the beginning of the postseason excitement, though. What followed was really something.

The Twins and NL champion Atlanta Braves engaged in a classic World Series. The Series opened at the Metrodome. Morris won Game 1 for the Twins, and Tapani won Game 2. The Twins got

Kirby Puckett reacts after hitting a game-winning home run in the Twins' 4–3, 11-inning victory over the Braves in Game 6 of the 1991 World Series.

a break in Game 2 when the burly Kent Hrbek, at first base for the Twins, pushed Atlanta's Ron Gant off the bag after taking a throw. Gant was tagged out. The Braves were furious.

The Twins lost the next three games in Atlanta, falling behind three games to two. Their backs were against the wall. Before Game 6, the always-optimistic Puckett shouted to his teammates, "Jump on my back, boys! I'm driving the bus today!"

It was Puckett's way of saying he was ready to carry the team. And he did. He tripled home a run and scored in the first inning. He leaped high against the glass wall in left-center field and robbed Gant of

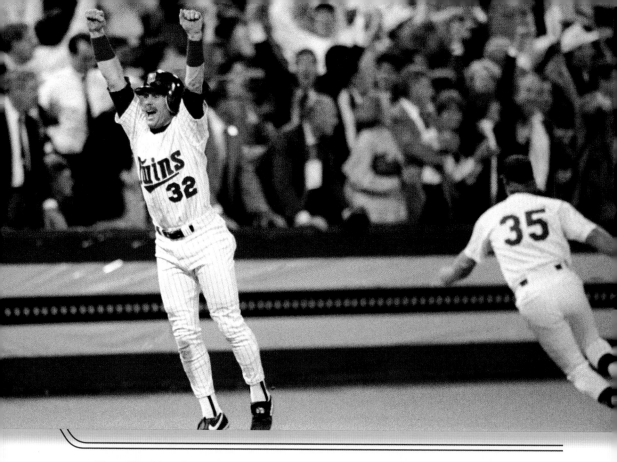

Dan Gladden leaps into the air once he realizes that he will be able to easily score the winning run in Game 7 of the 1991 World Series.

an extra-base hit in the third inning. He drove in another run in the fifth.

The game went into extra innings tied at 3–3. Then Puckett came to bat in the 11th. He teed off on Charlie Leibrandt's fourth pitch to him, blasting the ball over the left-field fence to give the Twins a 4–3 victory.

As loud as the Dome was in 1987, the noise this time might have topped everything. "And we'll see you tomorrow night!" shouted TV announcer Jack Buck to a nationwide audience.

If Puckett wore the Superman costume in Game 6, he must have loaned it to Morris for Game 7. Morris was a

Man of Steel for 10 innings in possibly the greatest Game 7 ever played. Morris and three Atlanta pitchers locked up in a scoreless duel through nine innings.

Kelly wanted to take Morris out of the game to start the 10th inning. Morris refused to leave. He got the Braves out 1–2–3.

In the bottom of the 10th, Dan Gladden doubled and was bunted to third. The next two Twins batters were walked intentionally. With the bases loaded, Gene Larkin, a part-time player, stroked a ball over the left fielder's head, and Gladden trotted in with the winning run. He stomped on home plate to give the Twins their second World Series title. Again, just like in 1987, the fans in the Metrodome crowd went wild, furiously waving their Homer Hankies.

The Metrodome

As a baseball park, the Metrodome was awful. It was built as a football stadium, a home for the Minnesota Vikings, and just happened to have baseball games played there, too. The original turf was springy, and balls would bounce like Super Balls over outfielders' heads, turning into inside-the-park home runs. Fly balls blended in with the Dome's gray ceiling, and locating them could be almost impossible. Opposing teams hated playing in the Metrodome. But the Twins made the most of their home-field advantage at the Metrodome. They won all eight of their World Series games held there in 1987 and 1991 on the way to winning titles those years.

The 1991 World Series had five one-run games and three extra-inning games. "How could the TV guys describe it?" Twins third baseman Mike Pagliarulo asked about Game 7. "[The Braves] had a chance to win, but they didn't. We had a chance to win, but we didn't. Then we did."

CHAPTER 6

SUSTAINED
SUCCESS

The Twins almost did not make it very far into the new millennium. After winning the World Series in 1991, the rest of the 1990s were like the 1970s for the Twins—miserable. They finished second in the AL West in 1992, then never came close to first place for the next eight years.

What happened? Some fans considered the Twins' owner, Carl Pohlad, to be a repeat of Calvin Griffith. They thought the billionaire was a cheapskate. But Pohlad said the Twins were losing money. He said he could not afford to pay big contracts to players. Jack Morris, the 1991 World Series hero, signed with the Toronto Blue Jays before the 1992 season. Kent Hrbek retired in 1994. The cruelest loss of all came in 1996, when Kirby Puckett had to retire because of a condition that made him blind in his right eye.

Tom Kelly retired as manager after the 2001 season.

Jacque Jones, *left*, and Torii Hunter, shown in 2002, helped turn around the Twins' fortunes. Major League Baseball had wanted to eliminate the team, but the plan did not work.

Worse yet, Major League Baseball (MLB) planned to "contract," or eliminate, two teams to save money. Pohlad told MLB commissioner Bud Selig that he was willing to let the Twins be contracted. But a judge ruled that the Twins had to live up to their contract to play in the Metrodome. The team was saved.

Then, something amazing happened. The Twins turned themselves around. General manager Terry Ryan had assembled a strong group. It included pitcher Brad Radke, catcher A. J. Pierzynski, infielders Doug Mientkiewicz, Cristian Guzman, and Corey Koskie, and outfielders Torii Hunter and Jacque Jones.

"We've arrived," Mientkiewicz said. He was right. In 2002, the Twins won 94 games and the AL Central title. The Twins beat the Oakland Athletics in the AL Division Series (ALDS) but lost to the Anaheim Angels in the ALCS.

Like Kelly, new manager Ron Gardenhire stressed good fundamental baseball. But he got along better with his players. Gardenhire's teams won six AL Central championships in his first nine seasons as manager. Ryan made a great trade in acquiring outfielder Shannon Stewart from Toronto to spark the club in 2003. But the Twins never could make a

Johan Santana pitches in 2004. Santana won the first of his two AL
Cy Young Awards with the Twins that year.

late-season deal that would put them "over the top" and into the World Series.

Still, the Twins were terrific in the 2000s. Johan Santana, a left-hander with a nasty changeup, won the Cy Young Award as the AL's best pitcher in 2004 and 2006. He was traded to the New York Mets in 2008 when the Twins could not re-sign him to a contract.

Eddie Guardado and then Joe Nathan were outstanding closers. More than anyone, though, the symbols of the Twins were the "M&M Boys"— Joe Mauer and Justin Morneau. Mauer, a catcher, won three AL batting championships in the

Former manager Tom Kelly, *left*, manager Ron Gardenhire, *right*, and ex-Twin Paul Molitor chat on October 4, 2009. Minnesota had just beaten Kansas City in the last regularly scheduled game in the Metrodome.

2000s. Morneau, a first baseman, became the Twins' most consistent home-run threat since Harmon Killebrew.

The Twins' division titles late in the decade were accompanied by drama. In 2006, they entered the last day of the regular season tied with the Detroit Tigers. Minnesota beat the Chicago White Sox at the Metrodome. Most of the crowd stayed put afterward. They watched on the Dome's big TV screen as the Tigers finished their game against the Kansas City Royals. Detroit lost 10–8 in 12 innings, and the Twins were division champs as the crowd roared.

The Twins finished the 2008 regular schedule tied with the White Sox for first place. But they lost 1–0 in a one-game playoff in Chicago for the AL Central crown. The only run came on a homer by Jim Thome.

In 2009, the Twins again played 163 games, one more than in a typical season. This time, Minnesota had finished tied with Detroit for first place. But this time, the Twins won the one-game playoff, defeating the visiting Tigers 6–5 in 12 innings. It was a fitting end to the Metrodome era. A franchise-record 54,088 fans cheered again as the Twins played their final regular-season game at their indoor ballpark.

The likelihood that the team's new outdoor ballpark, Target Field, would continue to bring in money for years

Playoff Struggles

The Twins visited the postseason regularly in the 2000s, but they did not fare very well once they got there. Their best playoff performance came in 2002, when they outlasted the Oakland Athletics three games to two in the ALDS. Minnesota then lost to the Anaheim Angels in five games in the ALCS. The Twins' four other trips to the postseason during the decade all resulted in ALDS defeats: in four games to the New York Yankees in both 2003 and 2004, and then in three games to both the Athletics in 2006 and the Yankees in 2009. The trend continued into the next decade, as the Yankees swept the Twins in the ALDS in 2010.

to come allowed the Twins to spend more on players. Thome came over from the Los Angeles Dodgers and signed a one-year deal. To top it all off, the Twins signed Mauer, a St. Paul native, for eight years and $184 million.

The Twins had a memorable first season in 2010 at Target Field. The team drew more than 3.2 million fans.

JOE MAUER

Baseball has never seen a catcher like Joe Mauer.

Catchers play the toughest position on the field. With all the squatting and foul tips off of their bodies, and with the added responsibility of calling pitches, it is generally considered tough to be a consistently great hitter while playing catcher.

Mauer proved otherwise. He won the AL batting title in his third major league season, batting .347 in 2006. He won it again in 2008, batting .328. And he won it again in 2009, batting .365, the highest single-season average by a catcher in major league history. He also hit 28 home runs in 2009, got on base in almost half of his plate appearances, and won the AL MVP Award.

"My dream was to make it to the big leagues, and now that I'm here, I'm an MVP," Mauer said. "I can't really describe it."

Minnesota finished 94–68 and won the AL Central. The Twins did this despite losing Morneau for the season. The slugger suffered a concussion in July against host Toronto. He was sliding into second base when Blue Jays infielder John McDonald accidentally kneed him in the head. Morneau's symptoms, including dizziness, continued. The team kept him out for the season.

Without Morneau, the Twins relied on a balanced approach. Utility man Michael Cuddyer moved to first base to fill in for Morneau. Carl Pavano led the staff with 17 wins. Left fielder Delmon Young batted .298 with 21 homers and 112 RBIs. Mauer hit .327, and Thome slugged 25 homers. Nathan, the All-Star closer, missed the entire season because of an elbow injury. But Jon Rauch played

Joe Mauer, *left*, and Justin Morneau, the "M&M Boys," wait to bat in 2010. Morneau was the AL MVP in 2006, and Mauer matched the feat in 2009.

well in his place. Minnesota then bolstered its bullpen by acquiring Matt Capps from the Washington Nationals and Brian Fuentes from the Los Angeles Angels.

But despite all the optimism, the Twins again flopped in the postseason. They had home-field advantage against the wild-card New York Yankees. But Minnesota still was swept in three games.

Despite the difficult ending to the 2010 season, things were looking up for the Twins. With Mauer, the hometown hero, leading the way and a new ballpark drawing rave reviews and bringing in more fans and money for the team, the Twins' future appeared to be bright.

TIMELINE

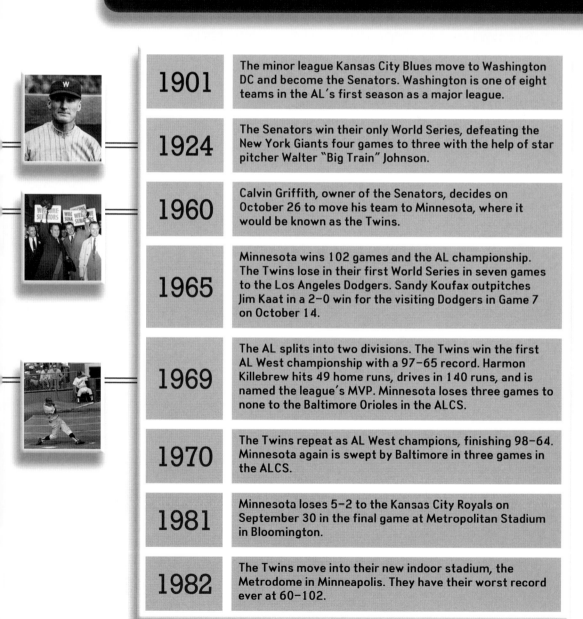

1901 — The minor league Kansas City Blues move to Washington DC and become the Senators. Washington is one of eight teams in the AL's first season as a major league.

1924 — The Senators win their only World Series, defeating the New York Giants four games to three with the help of star pitcher Walter "Big Train" Johnson.

1960 — Calvin Griffith, owner of the Senators, decides on October 26 to move his team to Minnesota, where it would be known as the Twins.

1965 — Minnesota wins 102 games and the AL championship. The Twins lose in their first World Series in seven games to the Los Angeles Dodgers. Sandy Koufax outpitches Jim Kaat in a 2–0 win for the visiting Dodgers in Game 7 on October 14.

1969 — The AL splits into two divisions. The Twins win the first AL West championship with a 97–65 record. Harmon Killebrew hits 49 home runs, drives in 140 runs, and is named the league's MVP. Minnesota loses three games to none to the Baltimore Orioles in the ALCS.

1970 — The Twins repeat as AL West champions, finishing 98–64. Minnesota again is swept by Baltimore in three games in the ALCS.

1981 — Minnesota loses 5–2 to the Kansas City Royals on September 30 in the final game at Metropolitan Stadium in Bloomington.

1982 — The Twins move into their new indoor stadium, the Metrodome in Minneapolis. They have their worst record ever at 60–102.

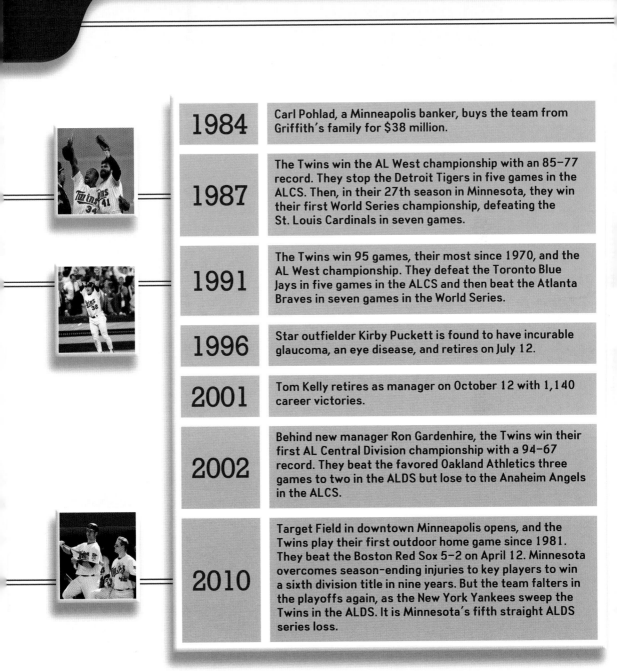

1984 — Carl Pohlad, a Minneapolis banker, buys the team from Griffith's family for $38 million.

1987 — The Twins win the AL West championship with an 85–77 record. They stop the Detroit Tigers in five games in the ALCS. Then, in their 27th season in Minnesota, they win their first World Series championship, defeating the St. Louis Cardinals in seven games.

1991 — The Twins win 95 games, their most since 1970, and the AL West championship. They defeat the Toronto Blue Jays in five games in the ALCS and then beat the Atlanta Braves in seven games in the World Series.

1996 — Star outfielder Kirby Puckett is found to have incurable glaucoma, an eye disease, and retires on July 12.

2001 — Tom Kelly retires as manager on October 12 with 1,140 career victories.

2002 — Behind new manager Ron Gardenhire, the Twins win their first AL Central Division championship with a 94–67 record. They beat the favored Oakland Athletics three games to two in the ALDS but lose to the Anaheim Angels in the ALCS.

2010 — Target Field in downtown Minneapolis opens, and the Twins play their first outdoor home game since 1981. They beat the Boston Red Sox 5–2 on April 12. Minnesota overcomes season-ending injuries to key players to win a sixth division title in nine years. But the team falters in the playoffs again, as the New York Yankees sweep the Twins in the ALDS. It is Minnesota's fifth straight ALDS series loss.

QUICK STATS

FRANCHISE HISTORY

Washington Senators (1901–60)
Minnesota Twins (1961–)

WORLD SERIES
(wins in bold)

1924, 1925, 1933, 1965, **1987**, **1991**

AL CHAMPIONSHIP SERIES
(1969–)

1969, 1970, 1987, 1991, 2002

DIVISION CHAMPIONSHIPS
(1969–)

1969, 1970, 1987, 1991, 2002, 2003, 2004, 2006, 2009, 2010

KEY PLAYERS
(position[s]; seasons with team)

Bert Blyleven (SP; 1970–75, 1985–88)
Rod Carew (2B/1B; 1967–78)

Goose Goslin (OF; 1921–30, 1938)
Kent Hrbek (1B; 1981–94)
Walter Johnson (SP; 1907–27)
Jim Kaat, (SP; 1959–73)
Harmon Killebrew (3B/1B/OF/DH; 1954–74)
Joe Mauer (C; 2004–)
Justin Morneau (1B; 2003–)
Tony Oliva (OF/DH; 1962–76)
Kirby Puckett (OF; 1984–1995)
Sam Rice (OF; 1915–33)
Johan Santana (SP/RP; 2000–07)
Frank Viola (SP; 1982–89)

KEY MANAGERS

Ron Gardenhire (2002–):
    803–656; 6–21 (postseason)
Tom Kelly (1986–2001):
    1,140–1,244; 16–8 (postseason)

HOME PARKS

American League Park (1901–02)
National Park (1903–10)
Griffith Stadium (1911–60)
    Known as National Park (1911–20)
Metropolitan Stadium (1961–81)
Hubert H. Humphrey Metrodome
    (1982–2009)
Target Field (2010–)

* All statistics through 2010 season

QUOTES AND ANECDOTES

"As long as I'm running this baseball team, we will play this game with respect. We will run every ball out, and we will give you a show every time we come out. Because that's what Kirby would have wanted us to do."
—Twins manager Ron Gardenhire, at a tribute to Kirby Puckett after Puckett's death in 2006

They say that what goes up must come down. But that is not necessarily true. Dave Kingman proved it on May 4, 1984, when he produced the strangest play in Metrodome history. Kingman, a powerful slugger for the Oakland Athletics, hit a pop fly that went up, up, up toward the Metrodome ceiling—and never came down. The ball went through a small drainage opening in a layer of the Metrodome roof. Twins infielders helplessly watched and waited for the ball to come down, but it was stuck. The umpires ruled it a ground-rule double.

When a bunch of good athletes come from one city or region, it is often said of that place that "there must be something in the water." Well, how about that water in St. Paul, Minnesota? Minnesota's capital city, located across the Mississippi River from the Twins' home of Minneapolis, is the hometown of four superstar players who have worn the Twins uniform. Paul Molitor and Dave Winfield, who were designated hitters by the time they joined the Twins later in their careers, are members of the Baseball Hall of Fame. They both picked up the 3,000th hit of their careers while with Minnesota. Jack Morris might have been baseball's best pitcher in the 1980s and has narrowly missed being voted into the Hall. And Twins catcher Joe Mauer is currently one of the best players in the majors.

GLOSSARY

acquire

To receive a player through trade or by signing as a free agent.

contract

A binding agreement about, for example, years of commitment by a baseball player in exchange for a given salary.

designated hitter

A baseball player whose only job is to hit. He does not play in the field.

draft

A system used by professional sports leagues to select new players in order to spread incoming talent among all teams.

fanatic

Extremely devoted.

franchise

An entire sports organization, including the players, coaches, and staff.

general manager

The executive who is in charge of the team's overall operation. He or she hires and fires managers and coaches, drafts players, and signs free agents.

jeered

Criticized nastily.

mammoth

Something huge or immense.

pennant

A flag. In baseball, it symbolizes that a team has won its league championship.

prickly

Easily irritated.

stratosphere

A high level of Earth's atmosphere.

watershed

Turning point; named for a point at which water drains toward different, larger bodies of water.

FOR MORE INFORMATION

Further Reading

Brackin, Dennis, and Patrick Reusse. *Minnesota Twins: The Complete Illustrated History*. Minneapolis: MVP Books, 2010.

Hoey, Jim. *Minnesota Twins Trivia*. Minneapolis: Nodin Press, 2010.

Puckett, Kirby, and Mike Bryan. *I Love This Game! My Life and Baseball*. New York: HarperCollins, 1993.

Web Links

To learn more about the Minnesota Twins, visit ABDO Publishing Company online at **www.abdopublishing.com**. Web sites about the Twins are featured on our Book Links page. These links are routinely monitored and updated to provide the most current information available.

Places to Visit

National Baseball Hall of Fame and Museum
25 Main Street
Cooperstown, NY 13326
1-888-HALL-OF-FAME
www.baseballhall.org
This hall of fame and museum highlights the greatest players and moments in the history of baseball. Rod Carew, Harmon Killebrew, and Kirby Puckett are among the former Twins enshrined here.

Target Field
1 Twins Way
Minneapolis, MN 55403
1-800-338-9467
http://mlb.mlb.com/min/ballpark/index.jsp
This is the Twins' home stadium. It was built for $545 million and opened in 2010. The team plays 81 regular-season games here each year. Tours are available when the Twins are not playing.

Twins Spring Training
Hammond Stadium
14100 Six Mile Cypress Parkway
Fort Myers, FL 33912
239-768-4210
Hammond Stadium has been the Twins' spring-training ballpark since 1991. It is part of the Lee County Sports Complex.

INDEX

About the Author

Joe Bissen is a sports copy editor at the *St. Paul Pioneer Press*. His writing has appeared in *Minnesota Golfer*, *Mpls-St.Paul Magazine*, and the *Duluth News-Tribune*. He lives in White Bear Lake, Minnesota, with his wife and three children. He has followed the Twins for 45 years.